The Pa

M000194120

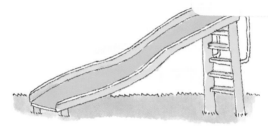

by Linley Stover   illustrated by Paul Harvey

Orlando   Boston   Dallas   Chicago   San Diego

Visit *The Learning Site!*

www.harcourtschool.com

ISBN 0-15-325414-9

14 15 16 17 18 19 20 985 10 09 08 07 06

Ordering Options
ISBN 0-15-323766-X (Collection)
ISBN 0-15-329533-3 (package of 5)

We go to the park.

We go on a bus.

We go to the park.

We go on a bike.

We go to the park.

We go on a train.

We like to go!